W9-AAR-285

A LITTLE BOOK OF POEMS & PRAYERS

A LITTLE BOOK OF POEMS & PRAYERS

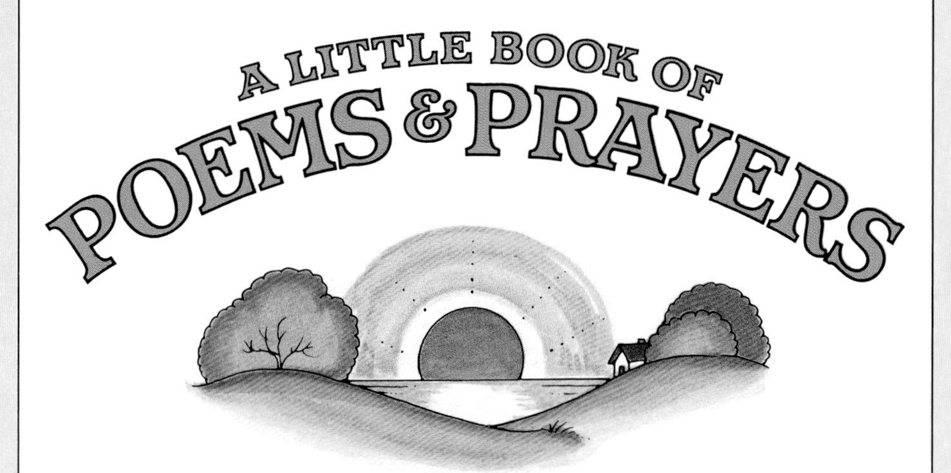

JOAN WALSH ANGLUND

Simon & Schuster Books for Young Readers

ACKNOWLEDGMENTS

We have made every effort to trace the ownership of all copyrighted materials and to secure permission from copyright holders. Any errors are unintentional, and corrections will be made in future editions wherever possible. Sincere thanks are due to the following publishers for use of copyrighted material:

Curtis Brown, Ltd. for "Morning Prayer" from *The New Nutcracker Suite and Other Innocent Verses*. Copyright © 1962 by Ogden Nash. Paul Hamlyn Publishing: Dean & Son Ltd. for "The Earth Has Got a Carpet" from *Lucie Attwell's Pop-up Book of Prayers*. Copyright 1974. Harper & Row, Publishers, Inc. and Harold Ober Associates Inc. for "Now Every Child" from Eleanor Farjeon's *Poems for Children*, originally published in *Come Christmas*. Copyright 1927, renewed 1955 by Eleanor Farjeon. Harper & Row, Publishers, Inc. and William Collins Sons & Co. Ltd. for excerpts from *A Gift for God* by Mother Teresa. Copyright © 1975 by Mother Teresa Missionaries of Charity. Macmillan Publishing Company for "A Summer Morning" from *Poems* by Rachel Field. Copyright 1957 and for "Night" from *Collected Poems* by Sara Teasdale. Copyright 1930 by Sara Teasdale Filsinger, renewed 1958 by Guaranty Trust Co. of New York. Smithsonian Institution Press for "Send Us a Rainbow" from *Nootka and Quileute Music* by Frances Densmore. *BEA Bulletin 124*. Smithsonian Institution, Washington, D.C. 1939, p.285. War Resisters League for "An Indian Prayer" from the 1974 WRL Peace Calendar, *As Long as the Rivers Shall Flow*. Western Publishing Company, Inc. for "A Child's Prayer" by Matilda Betham-Edwards from *Prayers for Children*—A Little Golden Book. Copyright 1974, 1952.

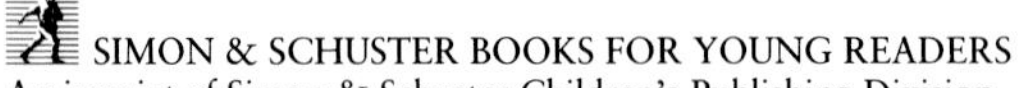

SIMON & SCHUSTER BOOKS FOR YOUNG READERS
An imprint of Simon & Schuster Children's Publishing Division
1230 Avenue of the Americas, New York, New York 10020.

10 9 8 7 6

Anglund, Joan Walsh. A little book of poems & prayers / by Joan Walsh Anglund. p. cm.
Summary: A collection of poems and prayers by such authors as Rachel Field, Ogden Nash, and Eleanor Farjeon. Includes anonymous pieces and quotations from the Bible. 1. Children's poetry. 2. Prayers—Juvenile literature. [1. Poetry—Collections. 2. Prayers.] I. Title.
PN6109.97.A54 1989 808.81'9—dc19 89-5914 CIP AC

ISBN 0-671-67115-4

For
Nana, Marguerite and Blanche…
with love,
and happy memories

This is the day
which the Lord hath made;
We will rejoice
and be glad in it.

Psalm 118:24

I saw dawn creep across the sky,
And all the gulls go flying by.
I saw the sea put on its dress
Of blue mid-summer loveliness,
And heard the trees begin to stir
Green arms of pine and juniper.
I heard the wind call out and say:
"Get up, my dear, it is to-day!"

Rachel Field

So here hath been dawning
Another blue day.
Think, wilt thou let it
Slip useless away?

Thomas Carlyle

Through the night Thine angels kept
Watch beside me while I slept.
Now the dark has gone away,
Lord, I thank Thee for this day.

William Canton

Now another day is breaking,
Sleep was sweet and so is waking,
Dear Lord, I promised you last night
Never again to sulk or fight.
Such vows are easier to keep
When a child is sound asleep.
Today, O Lord, for your dear sake,
I'll try to keep them when awake.

Ogden Nash

Now before I run to play,
Let me not forget to pray
To God who kept me through the night
And waked me with the morning light.
Help me, Lord, to love Thee more
Than I ever loved before,
In my work and in my play,
Be Thou with me through the day.
Unknown

Dear Father, hear and bless
Thy beasts and singing birds,
And guard with tenderness
Small things that have no words.
Unknown

He prayeth best, who loveth best
All things both great and small;
For the dear God who loveth us,
He made and loveth all.
Samuel Taylor Coleridge

Hurt no living thing:
Ladybird, nor butterfly,
Nor moth with dusty wing,
Nor cricket chirping cheerily,
Nor grasshopper so light of leap,
Nor dancing gnat, nor beetle fat,
Nor harmless worm that creep.

Christina Rossetti

All things bright and beautiful,
All creatures great and small,
All things wise and wonderful,
The Lord God made them all.

Each little flower that opens,
Each little bird that sings,
He made their glowing colors,
He made their tiny wings.

The tall trees in the greenwood,
The meadows where we play,
The rushes by the water
We gather every day—

He gave us eyes to see them,
And lips that we might tell
How great is God Almighty,
Who has made all things well!

Cecil Frances Alexander

Dear God in Paradise
Look upon our sowing:
Bless the little gardens
And the green things growing.

Unknown

The groves
were God's first temples.

William Cullen Bryant

For lo, the winter is past,
the rain is over and gone.
The flowers appear on the earth;
the time of the singing of birds is come,
and the voice of the turtle
is heard in our land.

Song of Solomon 2:11-12

. . . there shall be showers of blessing.

Ezekiel 34:26

There are three ways
children express
sorrow:
Some children cry,
some children are silent;
Wise children know
how to turn sorrow
into
song.

Hassidic

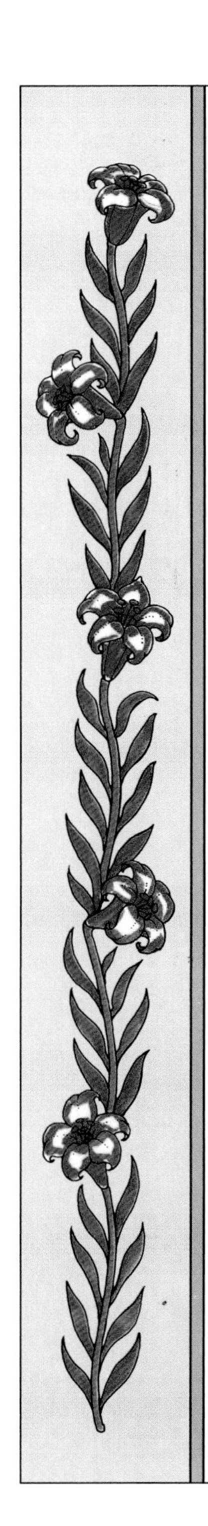

When someone is wronged,
he must put aside
all resentment
and say,
"My mind shall not
be disturbed;
no angry word
shall escape my lips;
I will remain kind
and friendly,
with loving thoughts
and no secret spite."

Buddhist Prayer

North, South, East, and West,
May Thy holy name be blessed;
Everywhere beneath the sun,
May Thy holy will be done.

William Canton

Whatever road I take
joins the highway
that leads to Thee.

Persian

Broad is the carpet
God has spread
. . . and beautiful the colors
He has given it.

Persian

Altar flowers
are of many species
but all worship as one.

Hindu

Heaven is a palace
with many doors,
and each may enter
in his own way.

Hindu

God made the world
so broad and grand,
Filled with blessings
from His hand.

He made the sky
so high and blue,
and all the little children
too!

Unknown

God is our refuge
and strength,
a very present help
in trouble.

Psalm 46:1

Are we not all children
of one father?
Malachi 2:10

For flowers that bloom about our feet,
Father, we thank Thee,
For tender grass so fresh and sweet,
Father, we thank Thee,
For the song of bird and hum of bee,
For all things fair we hear or see,
Father in heaven, we thank Thee.

For this new morning with its light,
Father, we thank Thee,
For rest and shelter of the night,
Father, we thank Thee,
For health and food, for love and friends,
For everything Thy goodness sends,
Father in heaven, we thank Thee.

Ralph Waldo Emerson

Every act of kindness
is
a prayer.

J.W.A.

When I am sick
and cannot play
Lord, be with me
on that day.
Keep me cheerful,
and brave, too,
Remembering other
children who
Are also ill,
perhaps in pain,
Lord, help us, all,
to health again.

J.W.A.

You, whose day it is,
Make it beautiful.
Get out your rainbow colors,
So it will be beautiful.

Nootka Indian

Dear God,
Fill my net with little fishes;
Fill my mind with hopes and wishes;
Fill my eyes with beauty, too;
Give my hands Your work to do.
But, most of all, dear Lord, above,
Fill my heart with Your sweet love.
J.W.A.

Let nothing disturb thee,
Let nothing affright thee,
All things are passing
God only is changeless.

St. Teresa, The Little Flower

Jesus, friend of little children,
Be a friend to me;
Take my hand and ever keep me
Close to Thee.

Walter J. Mathans

Walk, then, as children of the light. . . .

Ephesians 5:8

For you are all children of the light
and children of the day. . . .

Thessalonians 5:5

Serve the Lord with gladness:
come before his presence with singing.

Psalm 100:2

God, make my life a little light,
Within the world to glow;
A little flame that burneth bright,
Wherever I may go.

God, make my life a little flower,
That giveth joy to all,
Content to bloom in native bower,
Although the place be small.

God, make my life a little song,
That comforteth the sad,
That helpeth others to be strong,
And makes the singer glad.

Matilda Betham-Edwards

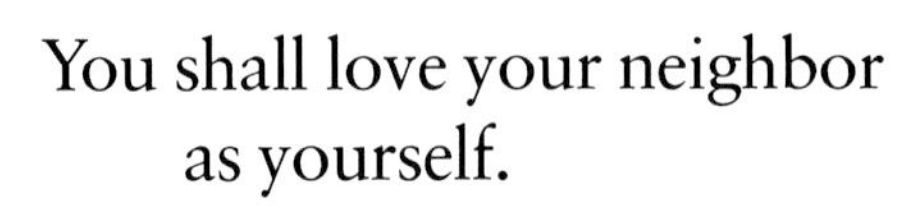

You shall love your neighbor
as yourself.

Romans 13:9

The earth has got a carpet
All shining fresh and green.
It's made of little blades of grass
With flowers in between;

And on this carpet,
Gay and free,
We dance our thanks,
Dear Lord, to thee.

Unknown

Thank you for the world so sweet,
Thank you for the food we eat,
Thank you for the birds that sing,
Thank you, God, for everything!

Edith Rutter Leatham

Peace be to this house
And to all who dwell in it.
Peace be to them that enter
And to them that depart.

Unknown

God, we thank You for this food,
For rest and home and all things good;
For wind and rain and sun above,
But most of all for those we love.

Maryleona Frost

Love is a fruit
in season at all times
and within reach
of every hand.

Mother Teresa

Give thanks to the Lord.

Psalm 106:1

THE LORD'S PRAYER

Our Father who art in heaven,
Hallowed be Thy name.
Thy kingdom come,
Thy will be done,
On earth as it is in heaven.
Give us this day our daily bread,
And forgive us our trespasses,
As we forgive those who trespass against us.
And lead us not into temptation
But deliver us from evil,
For thine is the kingdom,
And the power, and the glory,
For ever and ever. Amen.

O Great Spirit,
whose voice I hear in the winds,
and whose breath gives life to all the world:
Hear me! I am small and weak, I need your
strength and wisdom.

Let me walk in beauty, and make my eyes
ever behold the red and purple sunset.

Make my hands respect the things you have
made, and my ears sharp to hear your voice.

Make me wise so that I may understand the
things you have taught my people.

Let me learn the lessons you have hidden in
every leaf and rock.

I seek strength, not to be greater than
my brother, but to fight my greatest enemy—
myself.

American Indian Prayer

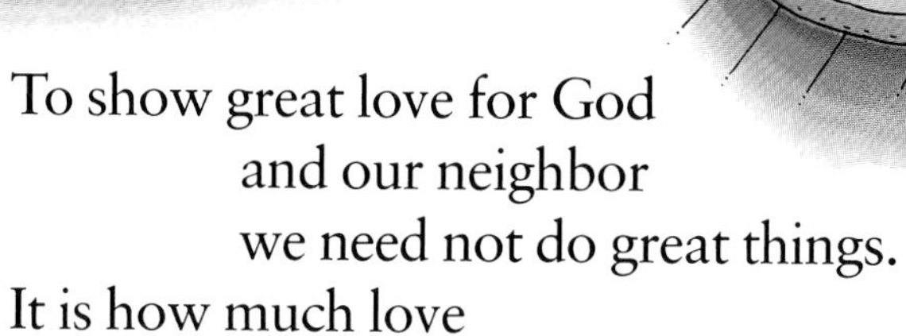

To show great love for God
and our neighbor
we need not do great things.
It is how much love
we put in the doing
that makes our offering
Something Beautiful
for God.

Mother Teresa

Every good gift and every perfect gift
is from above,
and cometh down
from the Father of light. . . .

James 1:17

Now every Child that dwells on earth,
Stand up, stand up and sing!
The passing night has given birth
Unto the Children's King.
Sing sweet as the flute,
Sing clear as the horn,
Sing joy of the Children
Come Christmas the morn!
Little Christ Jesus
Our Brother is born.

Eleanor Farjeon

What can I give Him,
Poor as I am?
If I were a shepherd,
I would bring Him a lamb.
If I were a wise man,
I would do my part.
But what can *I* give Him?
Give Him my heart.
Christina Rossetti

Sweet Baby Jesus,
though you're so small,
You've come here
from heaven
to bring love to all.
Dear Baby Jesus,
on this Christmas Day
open our hearts,
. . .and show us the way.
J.W.A.

Stars over snow
And in the west a planet
Swinging below a star—
Look for a lovely thing
And you will find it,
It is not far—
It never will be far.
Sara Teasdale

Lord, make me an instrument of Thy peace;
Where there is hatred, let me sow love;
Where there is injury, pardon;
Where there is discord, union;
Where there is doubt, faith;
Where there is despair, hope;
Where there is darkness, light;
Where there is sadness, joy.

St. Francis of Assisi

I see the moon,
and the moon sees me;
God bless the moon,
and God bless me.

Unknown

Matthew, Mark, Luke, and John,
Bless the bed I lie upon.
Four corners to my bed,
Four angels round my head,
One to watch and one to pray
And two to keep all harm away.

Traditional

Now I lay me down to sleep,
I pray Thee, Lord, Thy child to keep;
Thy love go with me all the night,
and wake me with the morning light.
Unknown